Portage Public Library

THE UNTAMED WORLD

Anacondas

Susan Ring

Chicago, Illinois

Copyright © 2004 Weigl Educational Publishers Limited

All rights reserved. No part of the material protected by this copyright may be reproduced or utilized in any form or by any means, electronic or mechanical, including photocopying, recording, or by any information storage and retrieval system, without permission in writing from the copyright owner. Requests for permission to make copies of any part of the work should be mailed to:
Copyright Permissions, Raintree, 100 N. LaSalle, Suite 1200, Chicago, IL, 60602.

Published by Raintree, a division of Elsevier, Inc..

Library of Congress Cataloging-in-Publication Data

Ring, Susan.
  Anacondas / Susan Ring.
    p. cm. -- (The Untamed world)
Summary: Describes the life, environment, and habits of anacondas, and the conditions that threaten them with extinction.
Includes bibliographical references (p.).
  ISBN 0-7398-6842-X (lib. bdg. : hardcover)
 1. Anaconda--Juvenile literature. [1. Anaconda. 2. Snakes.] I. Title.
II. Series.
  QL666.O63R56 2003
  597.96--dc21
                              2003006017

Printed in the United States of America
1 2 3 4 5 6 7 8 9 0   07 06 05 04 03

Project Editor
Heather Kissock
Raintree Editor
Jim Schneider
Design and Illustration
Warren Clark
Martha Jones
Copy Editor
Jennifer Nault
Layout
Bryan Pezzi
Photo Researcher
Ellen Bryan

Consultants
Jesus Rivas, Project Anaconda, Venezuela
John C. Murphy, Field Museum of Natural History, Chicago, Illinois
Mark Rosenthal, Lincoln Park Zoo, Chicago, IL
Acknowledgments
The publisher wishes to thank Warren Rylands for inspiring this series.

Photograph Credits
Aurora/Robert Caputo/IPN: pages 40, 56, 57; **G. Braasch**: page 10; **Bruce Coleman**: pages 4 (Erwin & Peggy Bauer), 41, 51 (Joe McDonald); **Corel Corporation**: pages 5, 25, 33, 38; **Dennis Desmond**: page 37; **Digital Vision Ltd.**: pages 27, 30, 31; **Cheryl A. Ertelt**: pages 11, 22, 28, 50, 61; **Getty Images**: cover (G. Braasch); **Bill Holmstrom**: pages 17, 18, 23, 29, 42, 43; **Photofest**: page 45; **Photo Researchers Inc.**: page 34 (F. Gohier); **A.B. Sheldon**: pages 6, 14, 60; **Tom Stack & Associates**: pages 7 (Erwin & Peggy Bauer), 16 (Joe MacDonald), 32 (Erwin & Peggy Bauer), 35 (Erwin & Peggy Bauer), 39 (R. Fried), 52 (Erwin & Peggy Bauer), 54 (Erwin & Peggy Bauer), 59 (Joe McDonald); **Visuals Unlimited**: pages 8 (Nathan W. Cohen), 9 (J. MacDonald), 20 (P. George), 21 (P. George), 24 (P .George), 53 (D.Yeske).

Contents

Introduction 5

Features 7

Solitary Species 17

Anaconda Young 21

Habitat 27

Food 33

Competition 39

Folklore 45

Status 51

Twenty Fascinating Facts 59

Glossary 62

Suggested Reading 63

Index 64

Introduction

> The anaconda has been feared throughout history by people of many cultures.

Early Spanish settlers in South America referred to the anaconda as matatoro, *meaning "bull killer."*

Deep in the rain forests and wetlands of South America lives one of the world's most exotic snakes. The anaconda has been the subject of many myths and tall tales. This snake has been worshiped as a powerful god and has been feared throughout history by people of many cultures.

Scientists are just beginning to discover how the anaconda lives. In this book you will find out what anacondas eat, where they live, and why they are so feared. You will understand why these snakes have suffered greatly, and how misinformation and greed have threatened their survival. Read on to learn more about the anaconda.

Anacondas live in the tropical rain forests of South America.

5

Features

> The two most common anacondas are the green anaconda and the yellow anaconda.

The yellow anaconda has a more colorful pattern than the green anaconda.

Anacondas are **reptiles**. The two most common anacondas are the green anaconda and the yellow anaconda. Green anacondas are dark green or brown in color and have large dark spots along their backs. On their sides they have large dark spots with light-colored centers. Yellow anacondas are similar, but their skin color is more yellow than green. The yellow color is brighter when the snakes are young. As the snakes get older, the color gets darker. Yellow anacondas have more spots than green ones, and their spots are smaller. The undersides of both types of anacondas do not have spots. Their bellies are either cream or light yellow in color.

Green anacondas have an orange stripe on their heads. This stripe goes from the corner of each eye to the jaws.

The green anaconda is found in the basin of the Amazon and Orinoco Rivers in South America.

7

ANACONDAS

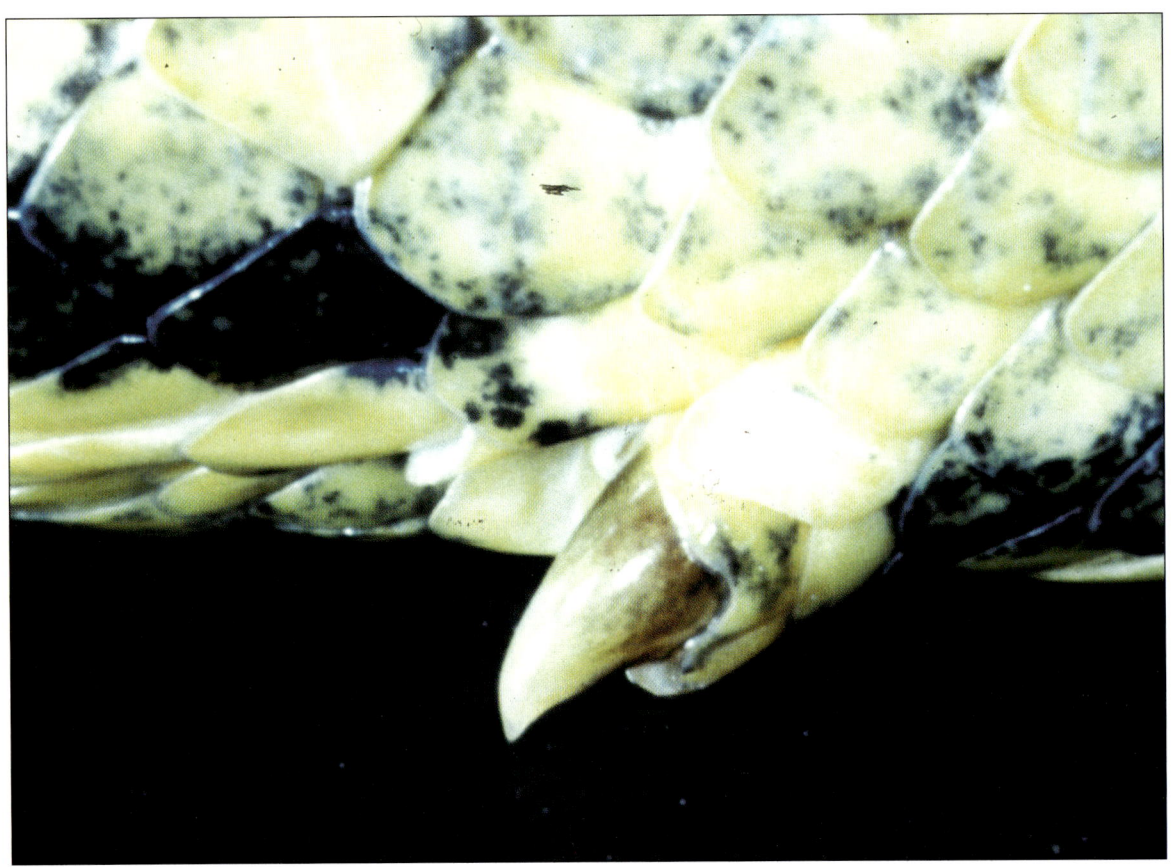

Anacondas have spurs near the end of their tails. These are thought to be the remains of limbs that anacondas have lost through evolution.

Ancestors

Scientists believe that snakes have been on Earth for more than 100 million years. For a long time, it was believed that snakes **evolved** from prehistoric lizards that had lost their legs due to a burrowing lifestyle. Some scientists now believe that different snake species may have come from different ancestors. This would explain why there are so many types of snakes in the world. Anacondas are semiaquatic, which means they spend much of their time in the water. This aquatic nature has led a few scientists to believe that the anaconda evolved from a water-dwelling lizard. Others believe that the anaconda did not develop from a lizard at all.

Classification

Snakes are divided into 11 different families. Anacondas belong to the *Boidae* family. Snakes of this family are not **venomous**. They kill their **prey** by **constricting** it. Snakes in the *Boidae* family have two large lungs. Most snakes only have one lung.

There are at least two species of anaconda. The two most well-known are the green anaconda and the yellow anaconda. Pythons and boas are other snakes in the *Boidae* family. Species of python include the reticulated python and the African python. The boa constrictor and the emerald tree boa are two species of boa.

Plants and animals are given Latin names. This is so that scientists around the world will call a species by the same name, no matter which language they speak. This naming system avoids confusion and helps scientists compare notes when they study. The Latin name used for the green anaconda is *Eunectes murinus*. The Latin name for the yellow anaconda is *Eunectes notaeus*. *Eunectes* means "good swimmer."

Emerald tree boas are found in the treetops of South American rain forests. Like anacondas, tree boas suffocate their prey.

Size

One of the most well-known features of the anaconda is its size. Anacondas are among the longest snakes in the world. Only the reticulated python grows longer. There is much controversy about the length of the anaconda. Some anacondas have been reported to be more than 37 feet (11.3 m) long, but the average length of the green anaconda is 16 feet (4.9 m). That is as long as a small bus.

Anacondas can be measured by placing a string along the length of a coiled snake's body. The string is then measured with a ruler.

With a circumference that can be up to 3 feet (0.91 m), the green anaconda is the heaviest snake in the world. A 20-foot long anaconda can weigh 250 pounds (113.5 kg). Some adult anacondas have been weighed at more than 300 pounds (136 kg). These snakes have most likely been female, since female anacondas grow to be larger than the males.

The yellow anaconda is considerably smaller than the green. The yellow anaconda has an average length of 7 feet (2.2 m) and can grow to be as long as 10 feet (3.1 m). Its average weight is only 15 pounds (6.8 kg).

LIFE SPAN

It is not known how long anacondas live in the wild. Anacondas that are kept in zoos live to be 20 to 30 years old. These snakes do not face the challenges of the wild. They do not have to survive dry seasons, lack of food, or hunters. Many animals in the wild do not live as many years as those that are taken care of in a zoo.

Body Temperature

Like all reptiles anacondas are cold-blooded. This means that their body temperature depends on the temperature of the air around them. If the air is cold, the snake's body temperature is low. If the air is hot, the snake's body temperature is high. Therefore, reptiles must bask in the sunlight to get warm and move to a shaded area to cool off.

Anacondas live in the hot tropical areas of South America. The temperatures are always high there because the tropics are close to the equator. This hot weather helps keep the anaconda's body temperature from becoming too cold. Anacondas use the hot morning sunlight to warm their bodies. They slide into the water when they become too warm. When there is little rain and the water levels are low, they slide under the cool mud to protect themselves when the heat becomes unbearable.

Anacondas are often seen in shallow water or basking nearby.

 ANACONDAS

Special Adaptations

Anacondas have some distinct features that have helped them survive for many years. Many of their features allow them to remain the most powerful hunters in all of South America.

Teeth

An anaconda's teeth are useful in the capture of prey. Aside from being very sharp, the teeth curve backward toward the snake's throat. The sharpness and shape of the teeth help the snake keep a firm grip on struggling prey.

The shape and angle of the anaconda's teeth help to keep prey from escaping the snake's grasp.

Jaws

One of the most impressive features of the anaconda is its jaws. An anaconda's jaws have highly mobile hinges that allow the mouth to open as wide as 180 degrees. At this width, anacondas can swallow animals almost twice the snake's own girth.

Tongue

An anaconda's tongue is its most important sense organ. Unlike humans the anaconda uses its tongue to smell and not to taste. When an anaconda flicks its tongue into the air, the tongue collects the various scents around the snake. The scents on the tongue are then transferred to the Jacobson's organ, a pair of sacs found in the roof of many reptiles' mouths. The scents are analyzed in the Jacobson's organ. Then the information is sent to the brain for scent identification.

Eyes and Nostrils

Since anacondas spend most of their time underwater, their bodies are adapted to water life. Their nostrils and eyes are located on the upper part of their head. This placement of their eyes and nose help the snake to see and breathe above water while the rest of it is submerged in the water.

When the anaconda brings its tongue back into its mouth, the scents from outside are transferred to the Jacobson's organ.

 ANACONDAS

Skin and Scales

Snakes, like all reptiles, have scales that cover their bodies. These scales are smooth to the touch. This is because a snake's scales are made of skin. The scales on an anaconda's underside are called **scutes**. The scutes are larger than the scales on other parts of the body. The snake grips the ground with its scutes when it moves. Every snake is born with a set number of scales. Throughout the snake's life the scales will grow in size, but the number of scales never changes. Each anaconda has its own special pattern of scales on its tail. This pattern is unique to each snake, much like people's fingerprints.

The colors and spots on an anaconda's scales are not only interesting to look at; they also help the snakes hide. Their dark coloring and skin patterns act as **camouflage** in the muddy water where they live. The snakes are almost impossible to locate from above the water. This helps them hunt for food without being seen.

Sometimes an anaconda's skin shows signs of rips or tears. These are its battle scars. The skin may become torn as the snake struggles to capture an animal for food, or as it tries to escape from an enemy.

Contrary to popular belief, snakes are not slimy to the touch. Unlike fish and amphibians, snakes do not cover their body with mucus.

14

FEATURES

Herpetologists Talk About Anacondas

Jesus Rivas

"This is the absolute master of the swamp, the custom-made animal for this place. It has evolved to catch and kill animals much stronger and much tougher than people."

Jesus Rivas is a **herpetologist** who studies anacondas in Venezuela. He and his wife, Renee, search the swamps of an area called the Llanos. Rivas began his work in 1992, and was the first person to study anacondas in the wild. Before he began his work, very little was known about these giant reptiles.

Bill Holmstrom

"Anacondas are very interesting animals. They are the top predator in their environment, and the largest snake in the world. They are quite unique and certainly worth saving."

Bill Holmstrom is the supervisor of the reptile department for the Wildlife Conservation Society in the Bronx, New York.

Jim Hitchiner

"The anaconda is the flagship species of South America. It represents an even bigger need—the need for all of us to preserve South America's wetlands and rivers...."

Jim Hitchiner is a herpetologist and the lead zookeeper of Tropical America at Roger Williams Park Zoo in Providence, Rhode Island.

Solitary Species

Anacondas are solitary animals.

A lone anaconda is better able to remain hidden from the view of potential predators and prey than a group of anacondas would be.

Like all snakes, anacondas do not travel or live together in groups. They are solitary animals. This helps greatly in their search for food. Due to their size, anacondas need a large amount of food to sustain themselves. If they all hunted together and had to share their food, there would not be enough to go around. So each anaconda swims, hunts, and lives by itself. The only time anacondas form a group is when males and females come together during mating season.

Hunting by itself helps an anaconda surprise and catch its prey.

Mating

When anacondas are ready to mate, they do something that is unheard of with most other wild animals. In many animal species, the males fight each other to win the attention of the female. Male anacondas do not do this. Instead, they create what is called a mating ball.

A female that is ready to mate sends out a powerful scent that male anacondas can detect from 3 miles (4.8 km) away. Males will then travel this distance to mate. When a male finds the female, he often discovers that he is not the first male to arrive. The female lies still as male snakes coil around her. There can be as many as 12 males in a mating ball, but only one female is ever involved. If there are many females in the area, fewer males will attach themselves to one female. The snakes can stay in this formation for 6 weeks.

When the female has finished mating, she slowly moves away. The males uncoil themselves and move back into the mud and tall grass.

A mating ball is a remarkable sight that has led to many stories about the anaconda having magical powers.

SOLITARY SPECIES

Viewpoints

Should anacondas be captured and kept in captivity for scientific study?

Not very much is known about the anaconda. This is unusual since there are many people who study snakes. Scientists find it easier to study jaguars, elephants, and even whales. They even know more about other types of snakes that are less secretive, such as rattlesnakes. How will scientists really learn about the true nature of anacondas? Should they be studied in zoos rather than in their natural habitat?

1 Anacondas live in such deep areas of the rain forest that it is difficult for scientists to study them. Keeping anacondas in captivity is the only way to study them over a long period of time.

2 By getting close to an anaconda and observing it day by day, scientists can understand its habits. They can also monitor its health and keep records of what these reptiles need to survive. Scientists can use this information to work with the snake in the wild and help save its natural environment.

1 Anacondas should be left alone in the wild. It is too risky to transport them and take them out of their environment.

2 Living in captivity does not adequately simulate a wild environment. The only way to really understand a wild animal is to keep it in the wild. There are too many other factors that interfere with the study of the animal when it is kept in captivity. In a zoo it does not hunt naturally for its food, it gets medicine when it is sick, and it does not face water or food shortages.

19

Anaconda Young

Anaconda young are born live. They do not hatch from eggs.

A female anaconda will give birth to several young at a time.

Unlike **mammals**, snakes do not care for their young. There is no parental care such as cleaning, grooming, or nursing. Some snakes watch over and protect their eggs before they hatch, but the anaconda is a kind of snake that does not lay eggs. Anaconda young are born live. Once the snakes are born, they are left to care for themselves. This is a dangerous time for the young anaconda. It is small and vulnerable to attack by other animals. Many of the young snakes do not live to adulthood.

Some newborn anacondas refuse food for the first few months of life.

21

Pregnancy

A female anaconda's **gestation period** ranges between 3 and 9 months, depending on the temperature. Air temperature not only regulates the anaconda's body heat, it also affects the babies growing inside the mother. Warm temperatures speed up their rate of growth, while cool temperatures slow the growth rate down. A female can actually control the development rate of her young. She can bask in the sunlight to speed up their growth, or submerge herself in water to slow their growth. This is one way that the babies can get a good beginning in life. They can be born when food is more plentiful, rain is heavier, and temperatures are more bearable.

While the female is carrying her young, she weighs more than usual. This makes her slower and far more vulnerable to predators. She also has less room in her body for food. The female may stop eating until she gives birth.

Female anacondas often bask on logs to regulate their temperature.

ANACONDA YOUNG

Shortly after birth an anaconda leaves its mother and begins its independent life.

Birth

Most snakes lay eggs, but anacondas are born live. The babies develop inside the mother in eggs that are soft and clear. While developing the babies feed on the yolks of their eggs. They break out of the eggs while they are still inside the mother. It takes about 6 to 9 months for them to develop before they are ready to be born. The mother normally goes to a secluded area when she is ready to give birth.

Anaconda babies are born in a group called a litter. Larger females have more babies in a litter than smaller females do. There can be 10 to 80 babies born at one time. The offspring can be 1 to 2 feet (0.3 to 0.6 m) long when they are born. Some can be larger, measuring up to 4 feet (1.2 m) long.

Scientists do not know if the babies are the offspring of several of the males in the mating ball or just one. Scientists are comparing the **DNA** of the offspring and of the snakes in the wild to find the answer.

Mother anacondas do not care for their babies once they are born. The babies are independent at birth and must learn to hunt and protect themselves.

Development

Birth to 3 Years

At birth anacondas are only about 1 to 2 feet (0.3 to 0.6 m) long. The size of the mother determines the size of the young. Larger females have larger young. Young anacondas attract **predators**, such as the jaguar and the alligator. As a defense against these animals, a young anaconda can swim, hunt, and care for itself within hours of its birth. Still, many young do not live to maturity.

From the time they are born until they are about 3 years of age, there is much growing to do, and anacondas grow rapidly. As the snakes grow in size, they outgrow their skin. When this happens, they shed their skin, leaving it behind as new skin takes its place. Baby anacondas shed their skin for the first time when they are about 1 week old.

3+ Years

Anacondas that have lived through their first 3 years of life will have completed most of their growing during that time. By the time anacondas are 3 or 4 years of age, they have reached maturity and will begin mating. They still continue to grow because snakes continue to grow their entire lives. However, they now grow at a much slower rate and shed their skin less often.

Young anacondas feed on mice, rats, chicks, frogs, and fish.

Young anacondas fall prey to animals such as the caiman, a relative of the alligator.

Dangers Facing the Young

Baby anacondas face great challenges. They are independent from the minute they are born. It will take time and luck for the babies to become powerful, giant reptiles. As babies these snakes face many dangers and threats.

It is helpful that the babies are born with the ability to swim. This ability allows them to quickly escape from danger. Some, however, do not escape. Many baby anacondas do not reach adulthood, often dying in their first few months of life. They fall victim to other animals in the area. Animals such as caimans and ocelots, who would not dare to attack an adult anaconda, find the young to be easy prey. Many baby snakes must be born so that just one or two will live to adulthood.

Distribution of Yellow and Green Anacondas

Habitat

Anacondas are drawn to marshes, rivers, streams, and swamps at low elevations.

Anacondas are found in most South American countries.

Anacondas live in the tropical rain forests of South America. They can be found along the Amazon River in Brazil and in other wet areas, such as swamps and streams. Green anacondas are found in Colombia, Venezuela, Guyana, Suriname, French Guiana, Ecuador, Peru, Brazil, and Bolivia. They also live on the island of Trinidad. The yellow anaconda lives in Bolivia and Brazil as well, but is also found in Paraguay and Argentina.

Anacondas are drawn to marshes, rivers, streams, and swamps at low elevations. Sometimes anacondas are called water boas because they live their lives in and near water.

Tropical rain forests provide an ideal habitat for anacondas.

Home Range

An anaconda's **home range** is dependent on the seasons. During the flood and rainy season, the anaconda will be quite mobile because the rivers and streams are teeming with water. Its territory at this time will be about 0.1 square miles (0.3 sq. km). When the dry season arrives, the anaconda must stay in shallow pools. This limits its range to about 0.08 square miles (0.2 sq. km).

When the seasons change, the anaconda's home range changes as well. The snake has both a rainy-season home and a dry-season home. The distance between these homes can be as much 3 miles (4.8 km).

Anacondas are more often found in calm waters, such as swamps, than in fast-moving rivers.

Seasonal Activities

Unlike many other places in the world, the areas around the equator only have two seasons, rainy and dry. The rainy season is a time when it rains day after day. The rain brings plenty of water, filling up rivers and streams. Anacondas thrive during the rainy season. They live in and around slow-moving rivers and streams where they can stay cool and remain hidden while they are hunting. The rain also makes grasses and flowers grow, so the animals have plenty of plants to eat. This means that there are plenty of animals for anacondas to eat.

Mud puddles provide some moisture for anacondas during the dry season.

The rainy season does not last all year in the Amazon. When the dry season comes, what were once huge areas of wetland become dry, muddy pools. As weeks go by, anacondas spend their days searching for moist ground or small puddles to lie in. During the dry season, snakes find it more difficult to find these places. Sometimes they have to burrow in the mud in order to survive. Many animals do not live through the dry season. The Sun is too hot, and water is too scarce.

The Disappearing Rain Forest

Land Development

Even if no one ever hunted or killed an anaconda again, these snakes would still face a great threat. The land they call home, the rain forest along the Amazon, is being destroyed. Anacondas need to live in open spaces that provide them with the large animals they eat. Caimans, capybaras, and large birds are among the creatures that live in the rain forests and serve as food for anacondas.

The human population is growing more rapidly every year. As the population grows, so does the size of the cities and towns in which people live. Many of these cities and towns are expanding outward into areas that are home to very unique types of wildlife. The swamps and rivers in which the anaconda lives are being drained and filled with dirt for houses and office buildings. Over time the anaconda's home will shrink and may eventually disappear.

The most popular conservation programs aim to preserve the rain forests while still focusing on the economics of the people and countries in which the forests are found.

HABITAT

Deforestation

Along with development of new businesses and homes, the rain forest is also being affected by the lumber and farming industries. Scientists estimate that, in the early 1990s, about 35 million acres (14 million hectares) of Earth's rain forests were destroyed each year. Human activity is a leading cause of this habitat destruction. Logging and oil companies often tap rain forest resources in search of hardwoods or petroleum. Trees are cut down to make furniture and houses. Once the land is cleared of trees, farmers plant crops. Where there was once rain forest, crops and livestock are found. As a result of such deforestation, scientists estimate that about 137 species of plants and animals become extinct every day. Since wild animals have less habitat, fewer are able to survive. The anaconda is one of the many animals whose habitat is being threatened by deforestation.

Parts of the rain forest are destroyed using the "slash and burn" technique in which a plot of rain forest is cut down, and any vegetation that is left is burned. The land is then used for farming.

Portage Public Library

Food

Anacondas are the largest predators in South America.

Anacondas share their habitat with many animals, including storks.

Anacondas are the largest predators in South America. Being predators, they hunt for their food. Anacondas eat meat, which means that they are **carnivores**. They feed on animals that also make their homes in the wetland areas. Caimans, which are South American relatives of the alligator, are prey for the giant snakes. Anacondas also eat birds that wade and feed along the shore, such as storks and cranes. Small mammals, too, cannot escape the anaconda's appetite. Deer, wild pig, and the largest rodent in the world, the capybara, are all food sources for this giant of snakes.

The capybara is found in South America, where it lives in areas around ponds, lakes, rivers, and swamps.

33

ANACONDAS

How They Hunt

Some animals chase their prey until it becomes tired. Anacondas do not do this. They are **ambush** feeders. Hiding in the murky water, they wait in silence for an animal to draw near. With a powerful, quick jolt, the anaconda lunges forward and bites its victim. It then coils its long, muscular body around its catch. The anaconda does not crush its prey. Instead, its tight squeeze suffocates and cuts off the other animal's blood supply. Within seconds, the prey dies from suffocation or lack of **blood circulation**.

The anaconda coils itself around its prey. The snake squeezes tighter every time its prey breathes out so that the animal cannot breathe in again.

How They Eat

Anacondas do not chew their food. Instead, they swallow their prey whole. They begin by swallowing the animal's head and gradually work their way down its body. Swallowing an animal head-first is easier for the anaconda, because the limbs of its prey fold naturally against its body. This makes the prey more compact so that it slides smoothly past the anaconda's jaws.

Anacondas occasionally eat very large animals. Their mouths must be able to open very wide to do this. The hinges on an anaconda's jaws are able to open as wide as 180 degrees due to the very elastic **ligaments** that connect its upper and lower jaws.

Muscles along the length of the anaconda push the prey into the snake's body. It takes about 8 hours for the snake to finish swallowing a bird such as a stork. The rest of digestion takes place over 2 more weeks. The digestive juices inside the snake's belly break down the entire animal. Anacondas can digest bones, feathers, beaks, and antlers. Every bit of the catch is used to supply the snakes with the protein and vitamins they need to survive in the wilds of South America.

After an anaconda eats a large meal, it sleeps for several days and digests its food.

The Food Cycle

A food cycle shows how energy in the form of food is passed from one living thing to another. Anacondas are part of the food cycle from the time they are born until they die. Throughout their lives, anacondas affect the lives of many other animals.

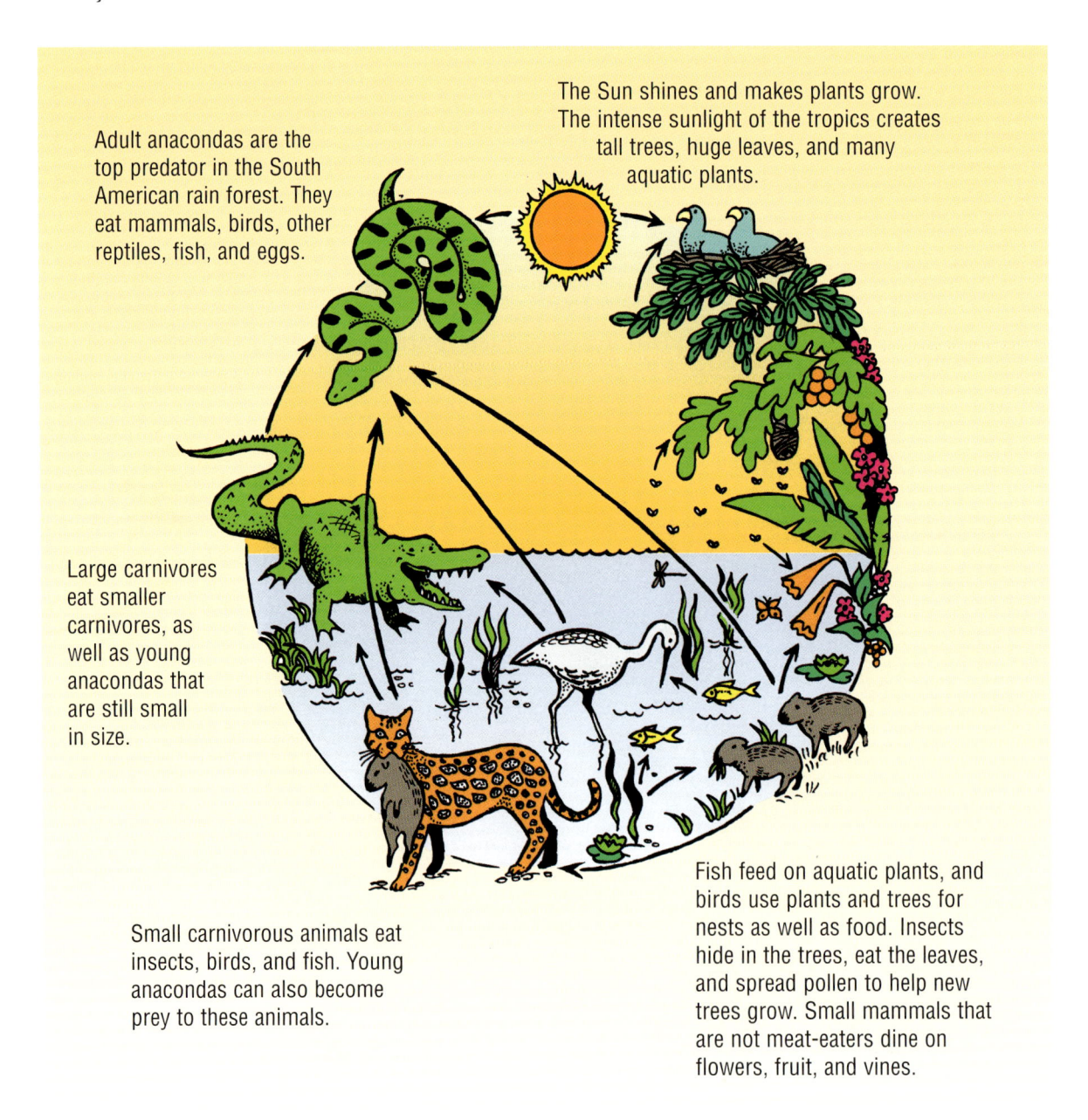

Adult anacondas are the top predator in the South American rain forest. They eat mammals, birds, other reptiles, fish, and eggs.

The Sun shines and makes plants grow. The intense sunlight of the tropics creates tall trees, huge leaves, and many aquatic plants.

Large carnivores eat smaller carnivores, as well as young anacondas that are still small in size.

Small carnivorous animals eat insects, birds, and fish. Young anacondas can also become prey to these animals.

Fish feed on aquatic plants, and birds use plants and trees for nests as well as food. Insects hide in the trees, eat the leaves, and spread pollen to help new trees grow. Small mammals that are not meat-eaters dine on flowers, fruit, and vines.

FOOD

An Anaconda Quiz

There are so many things to learn about anacondas. Do you think you can score well on this anaconda quiz? See how much you have learned already. Read the following statements and determine whether they are true or false. The answers are supplied at the bottom of this page.

1 Anacondas lay huge eggs.

2 The main threat to anacondas is the jaguar.

3 Anacondas swim in slow-moving rivers and streams.

4 Anacondas swallow their food without chewing it first.

5 Anacondas are most often found living alone instead of in a group.

6 In general, most snakes feel wet and slimy.

1) False. Anacondas do not lay eggs. They give birth to live young. **2) False.** The main threat to anacondas is the loss of their habitat. **3) True.** Anacondas are snakes that spend much of their time in the water. **4) True.** Even though it takes a while to digest, anacondas swallow their food whole. **5) True.** Anacondas are solitary animals. **6) False.** The skin of snakes and other reptiles feels dry and smooth.

37

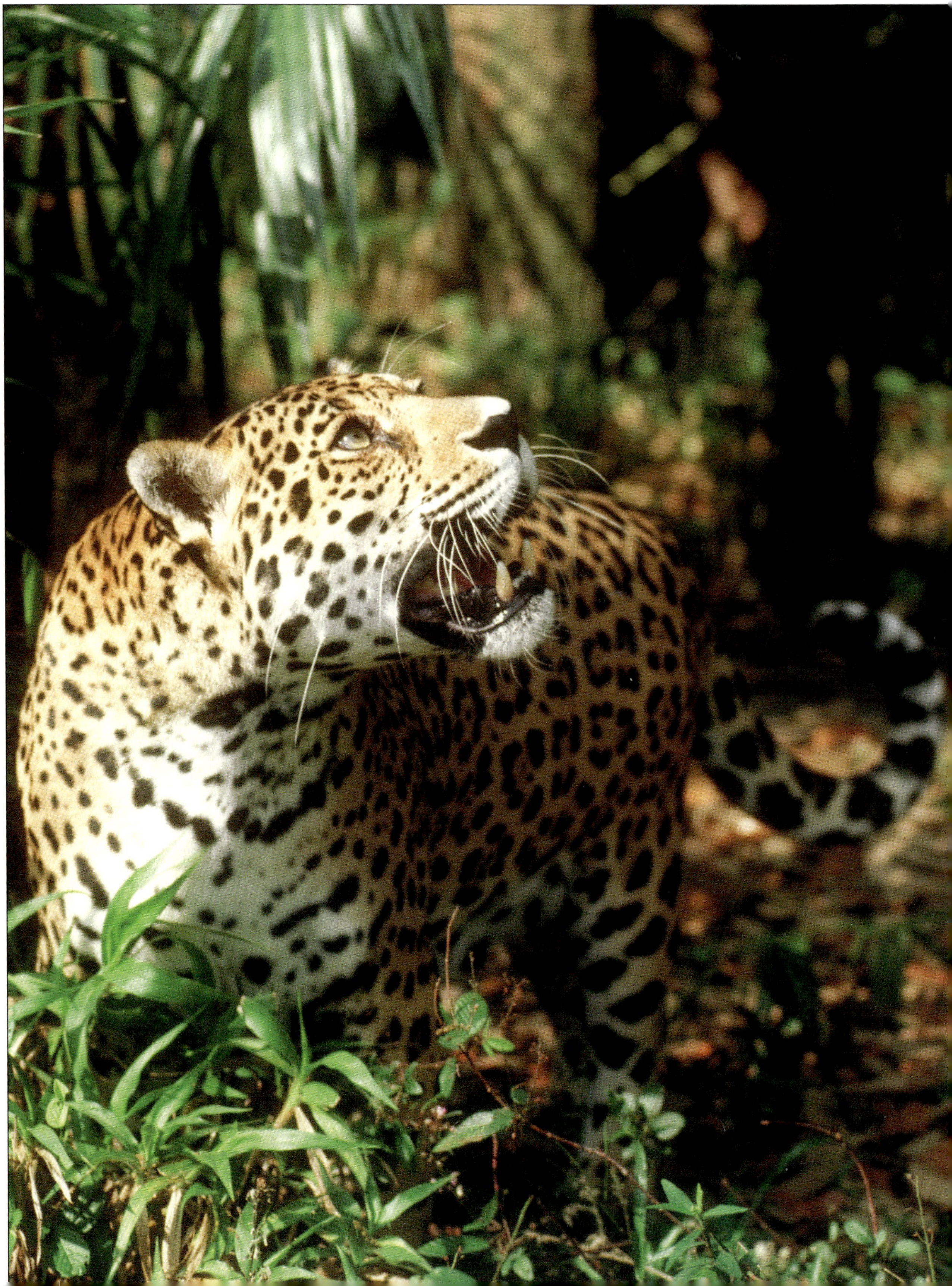

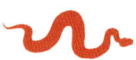

Competition

Anacondas have nasty tempers and do not run from conflict.

Jaguars are one of the many animals that share the anaconda's habitat.

Anacondas are the top predators of the South American wetlands. They can have nasty tempers and do not run from conflict. However, their main goal is to find enough food to eat. There are few large predators in the areas where anacondas live. Other meat-eaters, such as jaguars, are hunting for similar meals, but none can compete with the anaconda's strength and power. There are no other animals that would risk their lives to compete with an anaconda for the same meal. The only serious competition these snakes have is people. Humans are destroying their habitat, allowing less room for all the creatures that live there.

In addition to destroying the anaconda's habitat, humans also kill anacondas because they fear the snakes eat people.

Competing with the Environment

One of the biggest challenges to anacondas is the change of seasons. During the rainy season, the snakes are able to thrive. Once the dry season arrives, many die. During the dry season, the Sun is scorching hot and water is scarce. In some parts of the rain forest, the temperature can reach 130 °F (54 °C). Anacondas try to find protection in the mud, but many die from heat, lack of water, and exhaustion. Animals that the anacondas hunt also die in the dry season. They, too, cannot find food to eat or water to drink. This limits the prey available to the anacondas.

The dry season can be very harsh on the animals of the Amazon Basin, including the anaconda.

Competing with Other Animals

Being a water snake, the anaconda often winds its way down the rivers of the South American rain forests. These rain forests are home not just to anacondas, but to animals found nowhere else in the world. There are more species in a rain forest than in all the forests in the United States combined. The creatures that share the rivers and streams are no match for the anaconda. Caimans, capybaras, turtles, birds, and fish all fall prey to a hungry anaconda. Large cats, such as jaguars and ocelots, also compete for the same prey. There must be enough land to roam and hunt to ensure that there is enough food for all species.

After swallowing its prey, an anaconda will often return to the safety of the water.

While the anaconda may be a giant predator, it does have its vulnerable moments. Occasionally an alligator or large bird will eat a young, smaller anaconda. Adults, on the other hand, are vulnerable when digesting food. After an anaconda is finished eating, its body becomes thick, bulging in the middle. The snake moves slowly so that it can digest its food. It often lies in the water with a section of its belly floating above the surface. This is the time when the anaconda is most at risk of getting hurt by another animal on the hunt, such as a jaguar. Anacondas must be sharply aware of their surroundings and ready to protect themselves. They will sometimes make themselves disgorge their meal if they feel threatened. If given the chance, they would rather have the ability to escape than have a full stomach.

Competing with Humans

Humans are the only major threat to the survival of the anaconda. The rain forests in which anacondas live are being cut down at a rapid rate. These snakes are losing their homes. People want more land for farming and for building houses. As a result they are cutting forests down and clearing the land. Swamps and wetlands are being drained and made into farmland.

As farms spread across the area, the anacondas are sometimes found swimming in nearby rivers. The sight of the snakes can make the local people very afraid. They fear that the snake will eat the farm animals. Many times the snakes are killed. Other times, out of respect for the snake, the local people contact scientists to remove the snake and release it in another area.

Removing an anaconda from the water requires great skill. This is why even local people call scientists for help when there is a problem snake in the area.

Attacks on Humans

There are many more myths told about anacondas attacking humans than true reports. Although rare, humans have been attacked by anacondas. An anaconda will not attack unless it feels threatened or thinks the person is a prey animal. Some of the prominent biologists studying anacondas have been attacked during their field studies. In most cases the person was mistaken for a source of food. Anacondas are not poisonous, but they have very sharp teeth that can cause serious injury. Zookeepers and field biologists always work in pairs when handling an anaconda, not just because the snake is heavy, but because it has to be handled with extreme caution.

When handling anacondas, at least one person must hold the snake by its tail and another must hold it by the head to prevent the snake from biting or looping around someone.

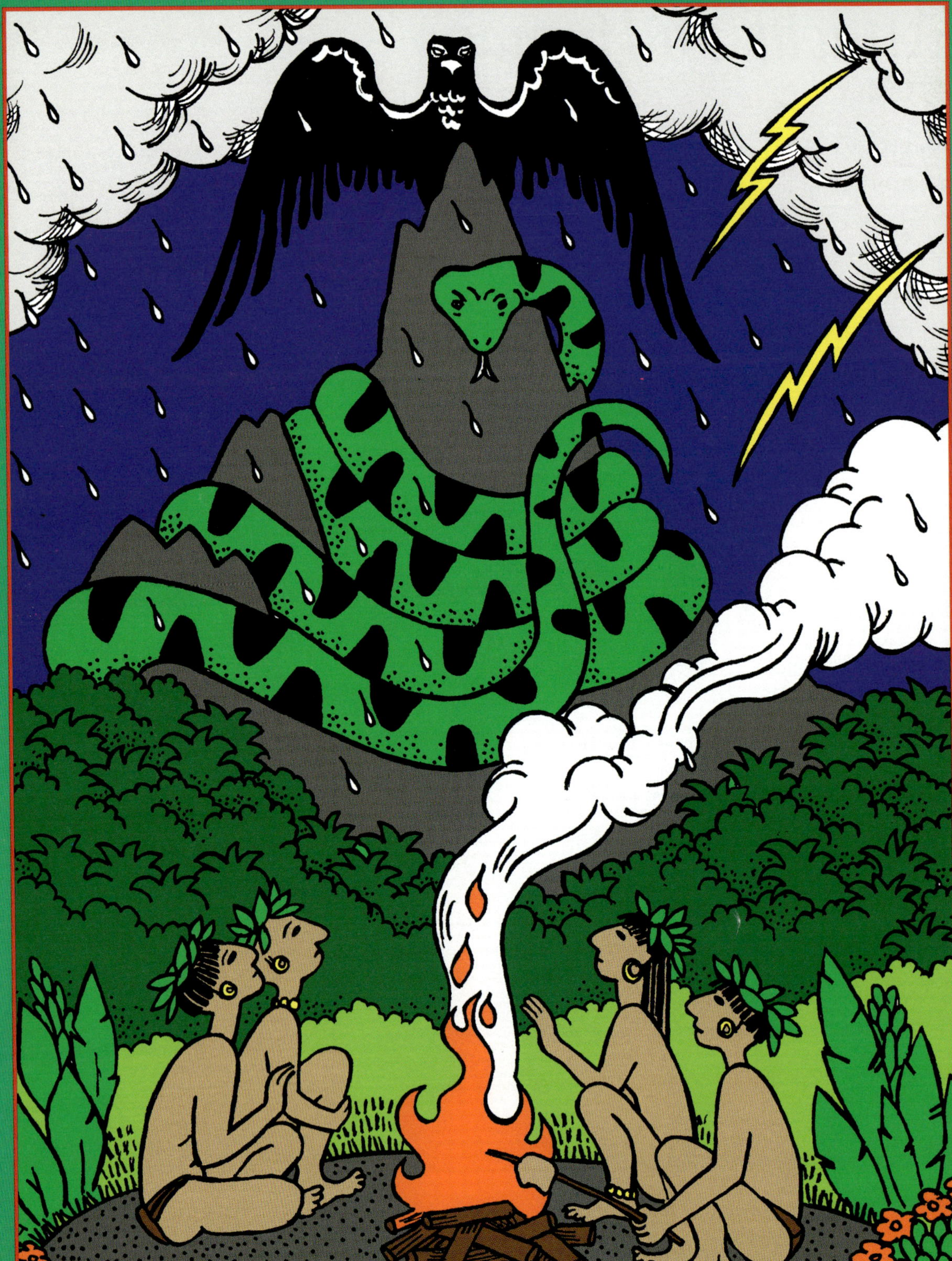

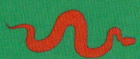

Folklore

Incorrect stories about anacondas should not be confused with folklore. Folktales are stories that people pass down from generation to generation. These tales help people understand their own role in the world along with that of the snakes.

Some native peoples who lived along the Amazon River worshiped the anaconda. They believed that, at one time, anacondas were harmful. They thought that a witch had put a spell on the snakes to stop them from harming people. Folktales from Venezuela and Guyana refer to a mountain that is guarded by a large eagle and an anaconda. When people began to light campfires near the mountain, they angered these guardians. The eagle and the anaconda created a tremendous rain to stop the campfires from burning.

In some folk tales, anacondas are believed to be protectors of the land.

The movie Anaconda incorrectly portrays the snake as a clever and vicious people-killer.

Folklore History

Many South American native groups connect strongly with the anaconda. Some believe the anaconda was responsible for creating the first humans. Others see the snake as a godlike creature that watches over them. These groups view the anaconda as part of their history and culture. One group, the Ceubo, believe that their ancestors were originally anacondas that became human when the snakes first shed their skin.

The Tukano combine their respect for the Amazon River with their respect for the anaconda. These people believe that they were first born at the mouth of the Amazon River. A boat shaped like an anaconda brought them down the river to their current home. Different elements of their culture, including songs and dances, were given to them during their anaconda-boat journey.

The Barasano people believe the anaconda is a guardian. While the eagle oversees the sky and the jaguar watches over the land, the anaconda guards the river and its inhabitants. The Barasano believe that each of these animals controls the passage from life to death among the other animals in their territory.

The Tukano are grateful to the anaconda for bringing them to their home on the Amazon River.

FOLKLORE

Myths vs. Facts

Anacondas eat people. — Anacondas have the potential to eat humans and probably have, but there has never been any record or proof of an anaconda eating a person.

Anacondas are naturally aggressive snakes. — These snakes usually choose to slide under the water and leave rather than meet up with a human. However, some snakes will defend themselves by biting in order to get away from a person trying to capture them.

Anacondas can never satisfy their appetites. — After eating a large meal, anacondas can go for months without eating again. They only eat an average of 2 to 4 times a year.

People often see anacondas that are more than 100 feet (30.5 m) long. — Anacondas have rarely been seen longer than 25 feet (7.6 m) long. Most anacondas are about 10 to 15 feet (3 to 4.6 m) long.

47

Folktales

Snakes have fascinated people for many years. They have been both hated and honored through the telling of folktales. In many stories, the snake teaches people a lesson about life, whether it is a lesson about greed, beauty, or trust.

The Snake and the Frog

A folktale from Africa tells the story of two young animals, a frog and a snake. One day, the baby frog decides to go for a walk in the jungle. Before he leaves, his mother warns him of the dangers he might face, including the deadly coils of the squeezing snake. The baby frog promises his mother that he will be careful and sets forth. He soon runs into a baby snake, and the two begin to play. At the end of the day, the snake hugs his new friend, and each returns home. The baby frog excitedly tells his mother about his new friend and the games they played, but the mother frog looks at her son with alarm. She tells him to stay away from the snake and to never receive another hug from him. The next day, the baby frog goes into the jungle once more. He encounters the snake again. Before he has a chance to run, the snake gives him a big hug, and the frog is no more.

The Snake Person

Another tale from Africa tells the story of a woman who gives birth to a snake. She loves the snake dearly, but when her husband sees it, he thinks it is ugly and tries to kill it. His wife stops him, asking that he spare their child's life. The husband agrees but is ashamed of this ugly creature. He decides to banish the snake to the forest where he will not have to look at it.

Years pass, and the snake grows into a handsome young man. He sends a message to his father and asks that he come to the forest for a visit. When his father arrives, he is shocked to see the young man before him. The two celebrate their reunion by throwing the son's snakeskin into a fire. As the snakeskin burns, it brings many riches to the father and son, and the family lives happily ever after.

The Water Snake

A story from Russia tells the tale of a girl who marries a snake, even though her mother is against the union. Three years pass. The girl is happy living underwater with her snake-husband, and the couple has two children. The girl, however, misses her mother and asks her husband if she can take the children for a visit. He agrees, and she travels to her mother's house. The girl's mother is overjoyed to see her daughter again and asks her many questions about her life with the snake. The daughter tells her mother about their underwater home and their happy life.

Before heading back to her family, the daughter and her children lie down to take a nap. While they are sleeping, the mother leaves the house with an axe in her hand. She goes to the water and calls to her daughter's husband. When his head rises out of the water, the mother swings the axe and kills him.

The daughter cries when she discovers what her mother has done. In her grief, she turns her own children into birds. She then transforms herself into a bird as well. The three fly away, never to be seen again.

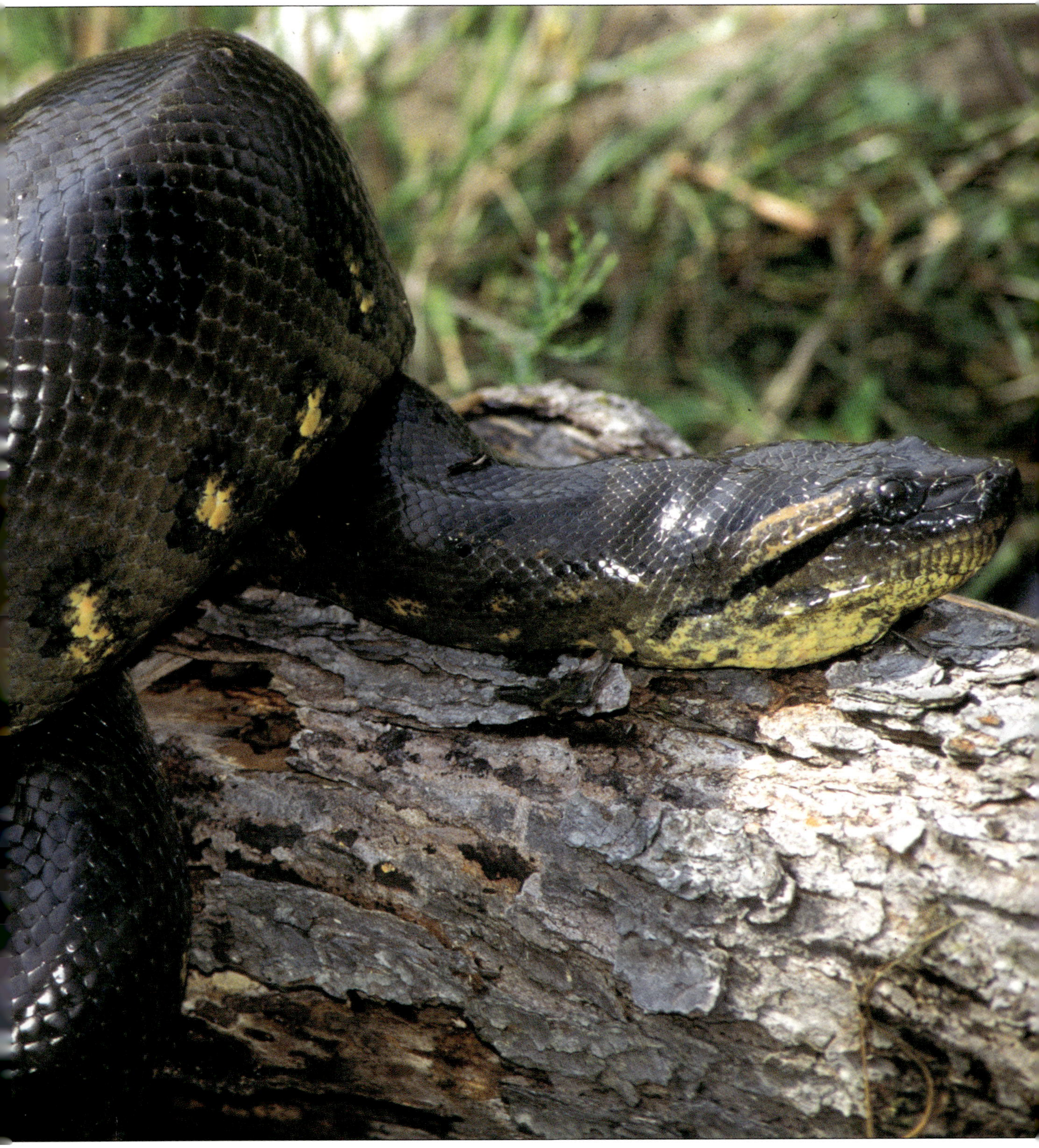

Status

> As more areas of rain forest are cut down, it is less likely that the snakes will survive.

Due to deforestation and land development, the anaconda's future survival is not assured.

Currently, the anaconda population is healthy and is not considered to be threatened. This situation could change in the near future, however. While baby anacondas face many threats to their survival, adult anacondas have no enemies other than humans. As more areas of rain forest are cut down, it is less likely that the snakes will survive. Deforestation and land development are critical factors affecting the future survival of the anaconda. This, combined with the sale of snakeskins to the fashion industry, leads to an uncertain future for the anaconda.

As more people begin to understand these giant reptiles, anacondas face two possible futures. The snakes could become more respected, and people may begin to protect these snakes and their habitats. On the other hand, the discovery of how and where the snakes live could also lead to their destruction.

The anaconda lives in a very specific habitat. As this habitat changes, so does the life of the anaconda.

By protecting the anaconda's habitat, people also protect all the other animals that live in the area, such as the white-necked heron.

An Uncertain Future

Due to its size and predatory nature, the anaconda is often misunderstood and greatly feared. Many people are not concerned about the uncertain future it faces. The anaconda must deal with its own natural challenges, such as changing weather patterns, as well as human-made challenges, such as the loss of habitat through land development. While the population is currently stable, it is constantly changing due to circumstances beyond the snake's control. Biologists are now taking steps to ensure the anaconda's future survival. Wildlife **preserves** have been created to serve as safe places for these wild animals to live and thrive. However, there is a race against time to save not only the anaconda but its habitat as well.

The Snakeskin Trade

Snakes have long been a source of fashion and have been killed for their skins for thousands of years. Snakeskin is used to make handbags, belts, watchbands, and shoes. The popularity of the snakeskin trade has led to concerns about the survival of many snake species, including the anaconda. In order to monitor the snakeskin trade, an organization called Convention on International Trade in Endangered Species (CITES) has established a **quota** program for countries that export snakes and snakeskins. Under this program, countries are only allowed to export a certain number of snakes and snakeskins each year.

Unfortunately, many snakeskins are exported illegally. In fact, over a 6-year period, almost 174,000 illegal snake imports were reported to CITES. This number included both live snakes as well as skins. Though not as popular as some other snakes, anacondas are still hunted for their skins.

Many countries, including the United States, Canada, and Britain, have laws restricting the import of snakeskin products.

Preserving the Pantanal

One of the places where anacondas live is an area called the Pantanal. This area is the largest wetland in the world. It is located on 140,000 square miles (362.6 sq. km) of land and covers parts of Brazil, Bolivia, and Paraguay. The Pantanal is fed by many rivers and streams, and floods during the wet season. At other times of the year, it is dry and gets little rain.

About 40 years ago, much of the wetland was drained, and houses were built on this land. Modern farm equipment began plowing the land, and many dams were built. This land development proved to be very destructive to the area, as it upset the **ecosystem**. A conservation organization called Ecotropica began working to stop the building of the dams and save the land and its wild inhabitants. Since 1988 Ecotropica has helped local people to work with the environment instead of making money by destroying it. They have educated people to develop a tourist trade that does not destroy the surroundings. This movement is a new industry called ecotourism. Ecotourism offers people the opportunity to visit a threatened area and to learn about the issues facing it. Ecotropica also participates in other efforts to save this area of land. More than 300 local organizations have joined Ecotropica to form a group called *Rios Vivos*. This means "living rivers."

The Pantanal is home to 230 species of fish, 650 bird species, 80 species of mammals, and 50 reptile species.

Viewpoints
Is ecotourism good for the environment?

Ecotourism is a growing industry all over the world. The belief behind ecotourism is that people will become more conscious of the environmental issues facing certain areas by being exposed to the problems firsthand. However, as the ecotourism industry gains popularity, more people are leaving their mark on land that is already at risk. This can have serious consequences for both the land and the wildlife that lives on it.

PRO

1 The more people are exposed to a natural area, the more they will grow to appreciate it and understand it. In turn, they will work harder to preserve these areas.

2 It is difficult to explain to someone why it is important to protect a single species without seeing where and how it lives. By traveling to an animal's homeland, its environment can be much better understood.

3 People who once hunted animals for a living have now become tour guides in their local areas. This brings money not only to the individual but also to the local villages. It provides a way for the people to have an income without feeling that they have to destroy the trees and animals in order to make a living.

CON

1 Along with more people, even ecotourists, comes more garbage. People can harm and destroy plants and riverbanks without realizing it. They trample on growing plants, scare wildlife, and alter a calm environment.

2 There are so many different animals in captivity and in zoos now that one does not need to travel to see them. Expert biologists can gather the information needed in a safe, controlled environment such as a zoo.

3 Not everybody who visits these places is honest. Sometimes people visit a rain forest or wetland in order to see how it can be exploited for personal or business purposes.

Project Anaconda

In 1992 an ambitious long-term study on the anaconda began. When complete the study, called Project Anaconda, should provide very detailed information about the anaconda, its lifestyle, and its habitat, with the hope of planning its future survival. Wildlife biologist Jesus Rivas is the field scientist responsible for the project. He and his wife, Renee, search for anacondas in the swamp areas in Venezuela called the Llanos. Rivas is the first scientist to study these giant snakes in the wild. Before he began his work, very little was known about anacondas.

Over the years, Rivas has studied more than 800 snakes. Currently, he is researching the breeding habits of the anaconda. Another goal of the project is to find out if anacondas can be raised in captivity.

Jesus Rivas and his wife are devoting much of their lives to studying the anaconda in its natural habitat.

STATUS

Tracking the Anaconda

Technology is playing an important role in the study of the anaconda. With the help of radio transmitters, scientists are learning more about the snake's biology, its home range, and its habitat use. More recently, radio transmitters have been used to study the breeding habits of the anaconda.

When scientists find anacondas in the wild, they fit them with radio transmitters. The snakes swallow the transmitters, which stay inside the anaconda for about 2 months before they pass through the snake's digestive system. This gives the scientists 2 months to track the snakes and compile information about them. The scientists follow the radio signals with a radio antenna. The information the scientists are gathering will help foster an understanding of this animal and its habitat.

By tracking anacondas, scientists have learned much about their mating and reproduction patterns.

What You Can Do

Anacondas are very important members of the animal world. You can learn more about these giant reptiles and other snakes by joining or writing to a conservation organization for more information. You can also let other people know what you have learned and spread the word about snake conservation.

Conservation Groups

INTERNATIONAL

World Conservation Union
Avenue du Mont-blanc
CH-1196 Gland
Switzerland

ECOTROPICA Brazil
Rua 03, n° 391
Boa Esperança -
78.068-370
Cuiabá, MT
Brazil

UNITED STATES

The Wildlife Conservation Society
2300 Southern Boulevard
Bronx, NY
10460

Society for the Study of Amphibians and Reptiles
Department of Biology
St. Louis University
3507 Laclede Avenue
St. Louis, MO
63103-2010

CANADA

Rainforest Reptile Refuge Society
1395 176 Street
Surrey, BC
V4P 3H4

Twenty Fascinating Facts

1 The speed at which anacondas lunge at their prey is 20 feet (6.1 m) per second. They look like a snapping rubber band when they lunge.

2 Anacondas can swallow an animal that weighs 80 percent of the snake's own body weight.

3 In 1978 biologist Bill Lamar was in Colombia, South America studying snakes. He saw one snake that was 25 feet long (7.6 m) and weighed between 300 and 400 pounds (136 and 181.4 kg).

4 New York's Wildlife Conservation Society offered a $5,000 reward for anyone who could catch a snake more than 30 feet (9.1 m) long. That was more than 75 years ago. The reward has been raised to $50,000. So far, no one has caught one.

5 Anacondas can hold their breath underwater for 10 minutes.

6 Anacondas do not have fangs. They have 110 teeth that are in rows. Their teeth are as sharp as fish hooks. The more the prey tries to break free and pull outward from an anaconda's bite, the more the teeth clamp down and grip tighter.

7 It takes only about 1 second for an anaconda to loop and coil around prey and begin its tight grip.

8 Anacondas sometimes swallow animals with quills, antlers, or horns without harming or puncturing their insides.

9 Anacondas have no ears, so they do not hear sounds the way people do. They feel vibrations through bones in their jaws.

10 In most species of animals, the male is larger than the female. In the case of anacondas, females are about five times larger than males.

11 An anaconda breathes through a windpipe located at the bottom of its mouth. This is how it is able to breathe while it is swallowing a large animal.

12 Anacondas make a hissing sound to defend themselves when they are threatened.

13 A snake's pupils are vertical like a cat's instead of round like a human's.

14 Large female anacondas have been known to eat smaller male anacondas.

15 Anacondas do not have eyelids. They have a clear covering over each eye for protection.

16 Humans have about 33 vertebrae along their backbone. Anacondas have about 400 vertebrae. Their joints are flexible, helping the snake twist and turn.

17 There are more than 2,500 different kinds of snakes in the world. Only a few hundred are venomous.

18 Anacondas are heavy on land, but they are strong, graceful swimmers in the water.

19 Once an anaconda has its meal in its mouth, it slowly swallows it whole.

20 Ninety percent of reptiles in the wild do not live to their first birthday because of the many dangers they face.

Glossary

ambush: To make a surprise attack

blood circulation: Movement of blood through the arteries and veins in the body

camouflage: Blending in with one's surroundings

carnivores: Animals that eat meat

constricting: Squeezing

DNA: Biological molecule that gives living things their features

ecosystem: All the living and nonliving things within an area

evolved: Developed and changed over millions of years

gestation period: Length of time that a female is pregnant

herpetologist: Scientist who studies reptiles

home range: Entire area in which an animal lives

ligaments: Bands of strong tissue that connect bones

mammals: Warm-blooded animals that breathe air and nurse their young

predators: Animals that hunt other animals for food

preserves: Areas set aside for the protection of plants and animals

prey: Animals that are hunted and eaten by other animals for food

quota: Limited quantity

reptiles: Animals that are cold-blooded, have scales and a backbone

scutes: Large scales on the underside of a snake

venomous: Able to inflict a poisonous bite or sting

Suggested Reading

Gerholdt, James E. *Anacondas*. Edina, Minn.: ABDO and Daughters, 1996.

Welsbacher, Anne. *Anacondas*. Mankato, Minn.: Capstone Press, 2001.

Murphy, John C., and Robert W. Henderson. *Tales of Giant Snakes: A Historical Natural History of Anacondas and Pythons*. Melbourne, Fla.: Krieger Publishing Company, 1997.

SUGGESTED VIEWING

Land of the Anaconda, National Geographic, 1998.

Killer Instincts: Anaconda, Giant Snake of the Amazon, Madacy Entertainment, 1999.

ANACONDAS ON THE INTERNET

One of the places you can find out more about anacondas is on the Internet. Visit the following sites, or try searching on your own.

Nashville Zoo
http://www.nashvillezoo.org/anaconda.htm

Jesus Rivas's Home Page
http://pages.prodigy.net/anaconda

Index

Amazon River 7, 27, 30, 45, 46
ancestors 8, 46

birth 22, 23, 24, 37, 49
body temperature 11

Convention on International Trade in Endangered Species (CITES) 53
classification 9
coloration 7, 14
competition 39–42
conservation 15, 30, 52, 54, 56, 58, 59

deforestation 31, 51
development 22, 24
dry season 10, 28, 29, 40, 54

ecotourism 54, 55
Ecotropica 54, 58
eyes 13, 60, 61

folklore 45–47
folktales 45, 48
food 10, 14, 17, 19, 21, 22, 30, 33, 35, 36, 37, 39, 40, 41, 43, 47, 59, 60, 61

gestation period 22

habitat 19, 27, 30, 31, 33, 37, 39, 42, 51, 52, 54, 56, 57
home range 28, 57

Jacobson's organ 13
jaw 7, 12, 35, 60

land development 30, 31, 51, 52, 54
length 10, 23, 24, 35, 47, 59
life span 10

mating 17, 18, 23, 24, 56, 57

Pantanal 54
Project Anaconda 56

rain forest 5, 9, 19, 27, 30, 31, 36, 40, 41, 42, 51, 55
Rivas, Jesus 15, 56

size 10, 17, 24, 36, 52, 59
skin 7, 14, 24, 37, 46, 49, 51, 53
snakeskin trade 51, 53
status 51–57

teeth 12, 43, 59

weight 10, 22, 59
wetlands 5, 15, 29, 33, 39, 42, 54, 55
wet season 28, 29, 54
wildlife preserves 52

young 7, 21, 22, 24, 25, 36, 37, 41

Portage Public Library

3181488850001 1

Ring, Susan
Anacondas
597.96 Rin

J
597.96
Rin

Ring, Susan

Anacondas

1/2007

Portage Public Library